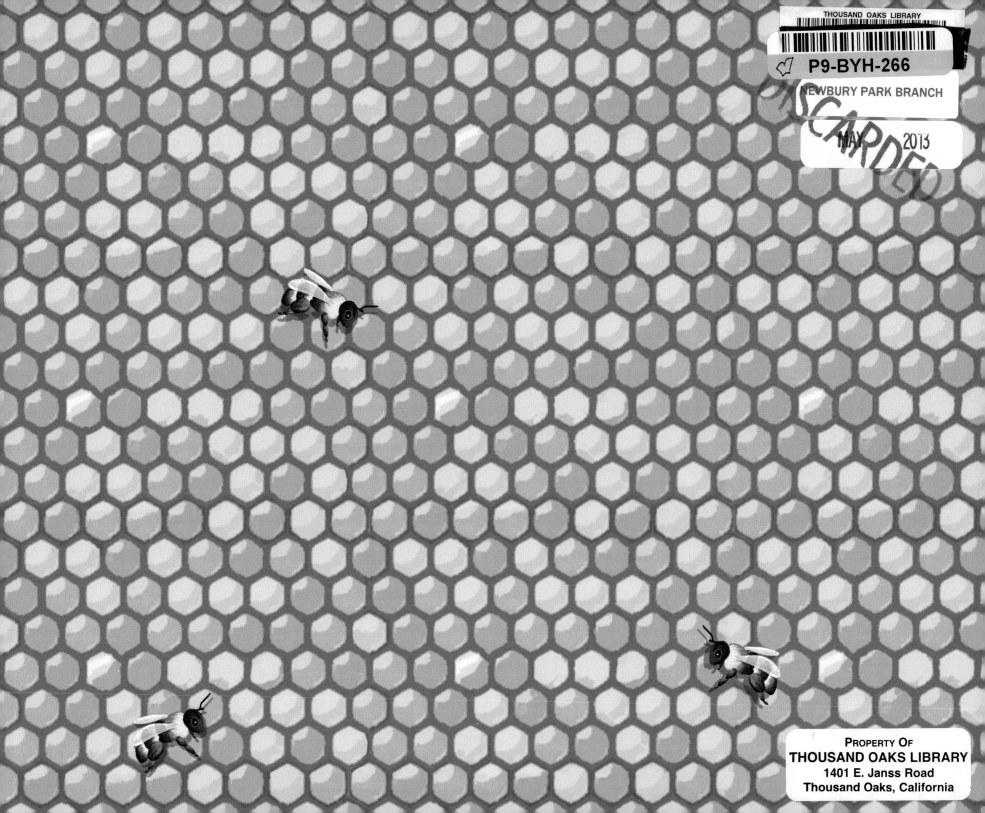

COLLECTION MANAGEMENT

THESE BEES COUNT!

Alison Formento   Illustrated by Sarah Snow

Albert Whitman & Company
Chicago, Illinois

**To Wandell Elementary School librarians Roberta Kleinbard
and Deidre DiMauro, who always buzz about great books.—A.F.
For my sisters, Megan and Nora.—S.S.**

Library of Congress Cataloging-in-Publication Data

Formento, Alison.
These bees count! / by Alison Formento ; illustrated by Sarah Snow.
 p. cm.
Summary: Mr. Tate's class visits a bee and honey farm, where Farmer Ellen teaches the children how to listen to the bees talk.
ISBN 978-0-8075-7868-1
(1. Honeybee—Fiction. 2. Bee culture—Fiction. 3. Beekeepers—Fiction. 4. Human-animal communication—Fiction. 5. School field trips—Fiction. 6. Counting.) I. Snow, Sarah, ill. II. Title.
PZ7.F6764Tgm 2012
(E)—dc22
2011008567

jj Fiction

The design is by Nicholas Tiemersma.

For more information about Albert Whitman & Company,
please visit our web site at www.albertwhitman.com.

Farmer Ellen led the class through a big field. There weren't any cows, horses, or sheep. There were only bees and tall flowers.

Mr. Tate's class loves taking field trips.
Today, their bus went to a farm.

Amy picked a flower and twirled it.

Eli looked around. "Is this a flower farm?"

Farmer Ellen smiled. "No, but we grow lots of wildflowers."

They walked through a grove of blossoming apple trees.

"Is this a tree farm?" Natalie asked.

"Trees grow here, too," Farmer Ellen said. "But at the Busy Bee Farm, we farm bees and honey."

"Honey tastes good," said Jake.

Eli held onto Mr. Tate. "Bees sting."

"Only when they're afraid or angry," said Farmer Ellen.
"And beekeepers always dress for safety before visiting the hives."

Farmer Ellen took everyone to a small shed.
Mr. Tate helped give out beekeeper gear.
The children pulled white jumpsuits over their clothes.

Shin smoothed the net over her face. "Here comes the bride!"

"We look like astronauts," said Jake.

"I feel safe in here," said Eli.

Farmer Ellen showed the class a field full of tall boxes.

"Welcome to the bee yard. These are bee houses or apiaries. Honeybees live here in hives. Most fly out each day to work."

"Bees work?" Jake asked.

"Yes, they collect pollen, which is tiny powderlike grains in flowers, for their food. This powder is carried on their legs to crops, flowers, plants, and trees and helps them grow. Sharing pollen this way is called pollination."

"Sharing's good," said Shin.

Farmer Ellen pushed a can with a long spout into a hole in the back of one bee house. "This smoker will help us see the bees." She squeezed the handle and wisps of smoke puffed out. Hundreds of bees followed the smoke trail and flew into the air.

Farmer Ellen said, "Now watch them work and hear what they say."

"Bees don't talk," Amy said.

"They do," Farmer Ellen said. "Listen to their buzz."

Everyone watched and listened. This is what they heard...

One by one, we zip up high,
buzzing through
the bright blue sky.

We fly over **two** waving dandelions, inviting us to visit.

We find **three** wild strawberries bursting with *sweetness*.

Four apple blossoms tickle us with soft petals.

Five
poppies
stretch
tall,
greeting
us
like
best
friends.

We stop for a drink where **six** farmhands water a crop of raspberries.

"Bees sure get thirsty," Jake said.

"*Sssh*," said Amy. "They're still buzzing."

We see **seven** clovers dance in the sunlight.

Eight *flowering cherry trees shimmer pink and white.*

In the garden, *nine* shiny peapods flutter in the breeze.

Before we fly home, **ten** tulips stand and nod, thankful for our pollen.

Buzzing, flying, working—we do more than you may know.
Each of us is nature's farmer, helping food and flowers grow.

"What did you hear?" asked Farmer Ellen.

"Bees count!" Shin said.

"Why else are bees important?" Mr. Tate asked.

"They make honey," Natalie said.

"Yes," said Farmer Ellen. "Bees drink nectar, a sweet liquid from plants, and carry it back to their hives."

"Why?" asked Natalie.

"Juice inside a bee's stomach changes the nectar into honey," said Farmer Ellen. "Bees spit the honey into a honeycomb made from beeswax. Then worker bees dry the new honey by flapping their wings faster than we can blink."

Jake and Natalie tried flapping their arms as fast as bee wings.

Amy knelt to watch a bee on a clover blossom. "Bees sure are busy!"

"Yes," said Farmer Ellen. "And without bee pollen, crops wouldn't grow, and we wouldn't have food to eat."

Eli said, "Bees are nicer than I thought."

Farmer Ellen smiled. "It's time to check the hives."

Everyone helped slide wooden frames
from the bee houses.
They found...
   one, two, three,
      four, five, six,
      seven, eight, nine,
         ten golden honeycombs.

Farmer Ellen said, "To get honey from honeycombs, we'll use an extractor. This machine spins honey out, which then flows into jars. We put a cap on tight and label the jar, all ready to take home."

Before the class boarded the bus to leave,
Farmer Ellen pulled jars from a crate.
"Would you like a gift from the bees?"

"Sweet!" said Jake.

"Thanks for honey, bees!" shouted Natalie.

"And for helping plants grow," said Shin.

A bee whisked past Amy's ear. She waved at it. "Buzzzzz to you, too!"

the buzz on bees

Every day honeybees travel from their hives to gather nectar and pollinate crops of food that we eat. They collect colorful dustlike grains of pollen from flowers and carry it in structures on their legs called pollen baskets. Some of this pollen rubs off bee legs onto the flowers they visit and fertilizes plant seeds so they grow. The rest is carried back to the hive and mixed with honey to feed other bees in the hives, especially the larvae or bee babies.

A huge variety of fruit, nut, and vegetable crops depends on honeybees. These include popular crops like apples, peaches, berries, melons, and citrus fruits, as well as broccoli, cucumbers, beans, pumpkins, cashews, and almonds. Even cotton plants used for making fabric are pollinated by bees.

With wings that flap over ten thousand times a minute, making them buzz, honeybees can fly up to five miles from their hives in search of plants and flowers to pollinate. They know how to find the way back to their hives because they practice. When first leaving the hive, honeybees take several short flights to learn their way home.

Watch bees outside a hive to see them fly in small patterns. A "round dance" is a circular movement and a figure eight pattern is what beekeepers call a "waggle dance." These dances are how honeybees share information with each other to help locate plants and flowers.

A typical hive, also called a colony, has thirty-five thousand to fifty thousand honeybees. A bee colony consists of a queen, drones, and workers. The queen's main job is to lay eggs—sometimes as many as fifteen hundred a day—and she can live three to seven years. Drones, who are male, fly out of the hive to mate with new queens and will die once mated.

Worker bees are females and do all the work for the hive even though they live only twenty to thirty days. When they are ten days old, a wax seeps from their abdomens in the form of tiny white flakes. Worker bees will chew these flakes to build the honeycomb, where honey is stored to feed the hive during winter months. Workers also guard the hive, pollinate plants, and gather nectar to bring back to feed the colony and to make honey. Worker bees will visit over two million flowers to make one pound of honey, and they can make sixty to one hundred pounds of honey in a year.

Honeybees have black and brown bands on their backs and are about one-half inch long. They are often confused with wasps or yellow jackets, which are more likely to sting than bees.

In recent years, honeybees around the world have been affected by colony collapse disorder, or CCD. This occurs when bees leave their hives, never to return. Without nectar brought home as food by worker bees, hives die off. Beekeepers, also known as apiarists, have been working with scientists to discover what is causing bees to disappear. One theory is that a virus or fungus may be affecting the natural ability of bees to find their way back to their hives. Use of pesticides on food crops is another possible cause of disappearing bees. Research continues to keep honeybees and their hives healthy and free from colony collapse disorder.

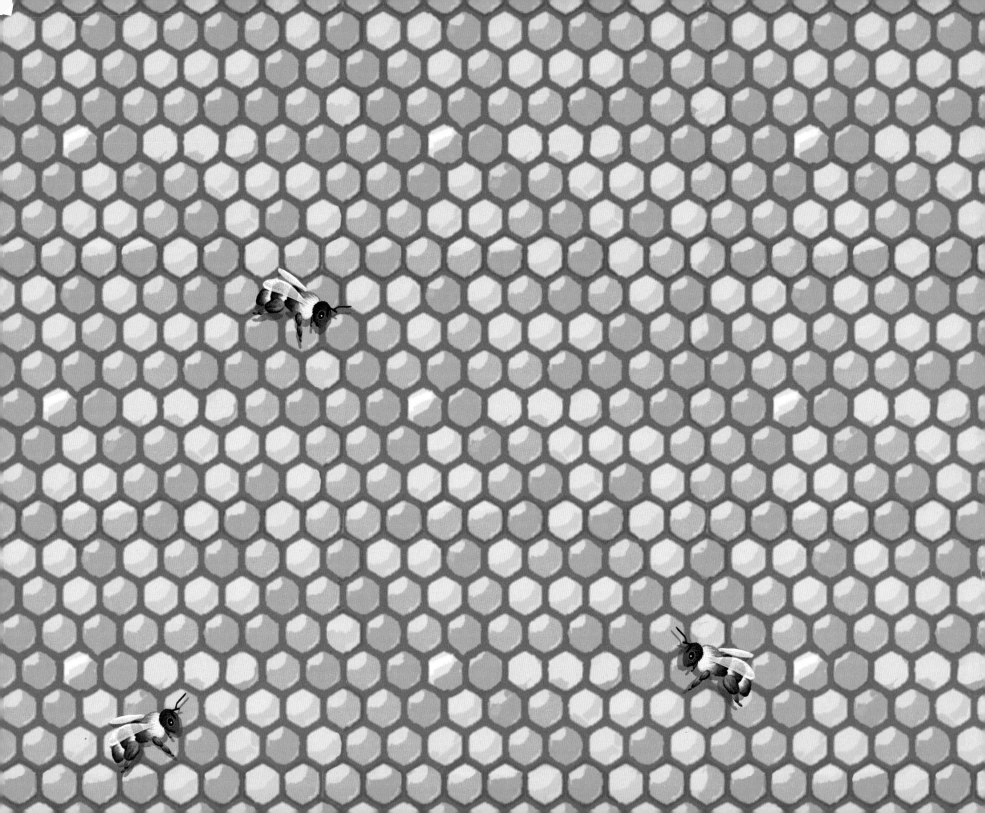